The Hatmaker's Wife

Lauren Yee

A SAMUEL FRENCH ACTING EDITION

FOUNDED 1830

SAMUELFRENCH.COM
SAMUELFRENCH-LONDON.CO.UK

FOR PRODUCTION ENQUIRIES

UNITED STATES AND CANADA
Info@SamuelFrench.com
1-866-598-8449

UNITED KINGDOM AND EUROPE
Plays@SamuelFrench-London.co.uk
020-7255-4302

Each title is subject to availability from Samuel French, depending upon country of performance. Please be aware that THE HATMAKER'S WIFE may not be licensed by Samuel French in your territory. Professional and amateur producers should contact the nearest Samuel French office or licensing partner to verify availability.

MUSIC USE NOTE

Licensees are solely responsible for obtaining formal written permission from copyright owners to use copyrighted music in the performance of this play and are strongly cautioned to do so. If no such permission is obtained by the licensee, then the licensee must use only original music that the licensee owns and controls. Licensees are solely responsible and liable for all music clearances and shall indemnify the copyright owners of the play(s) and their licensing agent, Samuel French, against any costs, expenses, losses and liabilities arising from the use of music by licensees. Please contact the appropriate music licensing authority in your territory for the rights to any incidental music.

IMPORTANT BILLING AND CREDIT REQUIREMENTS

If you have obtained performance rights to this title, please refer to your licensing agreement for important billing and credit requirements.

THE HATMAKER'S WIFE, under its current title, received its Off-Broadway premiere produced by The Playwrights Realm (Katherine Kovner, Artistic Director; Renee Blinkwolt, Producing Director) on August 27, 2013. The performance was directed by Rachel Chavkin, with sets by Carolyn Mraz, costumes by Michael Krass, lights by Amith Chandrashaker, sound design and composition by Ryan Rumery, props by Andrew Diaz, and dramaturgy by Alex Barron. The production stage manager was Lori Amondson, and the company manager was Evan O'Brient. The cast was as follows:

HETCHMAN . . . . David Margulies

HETCHMAN'S WIFE . . . . .Marcia Jean Kurtz

MECKEL . . . . .Peter Friedman

VOICE . . . . Stephanie Wright Thompson

GABE/GOLEM . . . . .Frank Harts

WALL . . . . .Megan Byrne

A MAN, HIS WIFE, AND HIS HAT, under its original title, was presented at the University of California San Diego's Baldwin New Play Festival in La Jolla, California (Naomi Iizuka, Head of Playwriting) on April 13, 2011 at the Forum Theatre. It was directed by Joshua Kahan Brody, with costumes by Eliza Benzoni, lighting by Sherrice Kelly, set and projections by Kathryn Lieber, original music and sound by Nicholas Drashner, and dramaturgy by Gabriel Greene. The production stage manager was Laura Zingle. The cast was as follows:

HETCHMAN	Daniel Rubiano
HETCHMAN'S WIFE	Natalie Bierriel
MECKEL	Matthew MacNelly
VOICE	Megan Robinson
GABE	Mark Christine
GOLEM	Kyle Sorensen
WALL	Claire Kaplan

A MAN, HIS WIFE, AND HIS HAT received its world premiere at AlterTheater. The production opened on November 12, 2011 in San Rafael, California, directed by Robin Stanton. Costumes by Jan Koprowski, lighting by Selina G Young, sound and projections by Norm Kern, original music by Daniel Savio, and dramaturgy by Nakissa Etemad and Elizabeth Williamson. The production stage manager was Mina Sohaa Smith. The cast was as follows:

HETCHMAN	Jeff Garrett
HETCHMAN'S WIFE	Patricia Silver
MECKEL	Ed Holmes
VOICE	Jeanette Harrison
GABE	Hugo Carbajal
GOLEM	Jon Deline
WALL	Nakissa Etemad

A MAN, HIS WIFE, AND HIS HAT was commissioned by AlterTheater, with support from Theatre Bay Area's New Works Fund, and was developed with the support of PlayPenn, Paul Meshejian, Artistic Director.

Special thanks to the El Gouna Writers Residency, Naomi Iizuka, Adele Edling Shank, Allan Havis, Antje Oegel, and the University of California San Diego.

CHARACTERS

HETCHMAN – Our hero. Hetchman the hatmaker. He wears a hat. Curmudgeonly.

HETCHMAN'S WIFE – Wife of Hetchman. Nondescript. Does she have a name? Who knows.

MECKEL – Hetchman's neighbor and only friend. Meckel is cheerful, popular, and kind. He is the opposite of Hetchman. He also wears a hat.

VOICE – A young woman.

GABE – Voice's boyfriend. Easygoing in a way Voice has never been.

WALL – A wall, probably female, that speaks with a quasi-Eastern European accent. The wall is realized in the play as an unseen voiceover. The actor playing the wall does not appear onstage. The wall's voice should emanate from a specific place (as opposed to a 'voice of god from above').

GOLEM – A golem, a la the Jewish golem of Prague. Only makes sounds but does intuit what is going on. Eats a lot. Made of mud and crap. Has a male presence. Can be doubled with **GABE**.

Note: **HETCHMAN**, *his* **WIFE**, *and* **MECKEL**, *despite being "old," are not necessarily old old. They are old in the way your math teacher could be fifty or ninety. Ageless. They also all speak with quasi-Eastern European accents.*

AUTHOR'S NOTES

Hatmusic is very important in this world. "What is hatmusic?" you ask. For you, I explain. When you are happy and you are wearing the right hat, you hear hatmusic. Hatmusic is indescribable and unique to each person, but think the clarinet section of Klezmer music.

For Goong Goong and Paw Paw

Prologue

(Living room)

(Lights up on a living room. In the center of the room is an old, musty easy chair, on top of old, musty carpet, from a color palette popular a long time ago.)

(Then **HETCHMAN** *on stage in his own light. He holds a hat out in front of him. A well-balanced man's hat. It is perfect.)*

(The hat has its own light. He puts it on. Together, they play the most beautiful music: hatmusic.)

(Another light up on **HETCHMAN'S WIFE**. *She looks at* **HETCHMAN**, *she looks at the hat.)*

(The hatmusic turns sour, tinny, grinds to a halt.)

Scene

(Living room)

(In the darkness, the sound of someone opening the front door, with some difficulty. The lights click on. We are in the same living room. **VOICE** *stands in the middle of the room with a large moving box labeled "pillows." She stares at the space, then she hears a human noise coming from behind the front door.)*

VOICE. Oh! Gabe.

*(***VOICE** *goes to open the door.* **GABE** *struggles with a much heavier moving box, labeled "books.")*

Sorry!

*(***GABE** *drops the box, exhausted.)*

GABE. It's cool. You were carrying all those – *(reads side of* **VOICE**'*s box)* pillows.

VOICE. I like packing by category.

GABE. Yeah, but box of pillows. *(re: his box)* Ton of bricks.

VOICE. *(shrugs)* I enjoy my books.

GABE. Well, thank god this is the last one.

VOICE. That's it?!

GABE. You want more?

VOICE. I didn't get a video.

GABE. Of what?

VOICE. Of us moving.

GABE. Why do we need a video?

VOICE. Do it again. Come through the door.

*(***VOICE** *takes out her camera.)*

GABE. Can I do it without the box?

VOICE. No.

GABE. I'm not getting the box.

VOICE. It's not going to look authentic without the box.

GABE. Yeah, 'cause it ISN'T. The moment has passed.

VOICE. It's important!

GABE. We're moving in together, not signing a peace treaty. There doesn't need be a historic record.

VOICE. It's kind of historic, right? I want to remember that this actually happened.

GABE. Then let me do it of you.

VOICE. Noooo.

(**GABE** *sits down in the easy chair, closes his eyes.*)

GABE. Fine. I'll do it in a minute.

VOICE. In a minute you'll be asleep. *(beat)* You're not asleep, are you?

GABE. No. Just listening.

(**VOICE** *joins him on the chair.*)

VOICE. To what?

GABE. The sound of space. Land.

VOICE. We're renting.

GABE. Still: LAND.

VOICE. Suburbia.

GABE. Fresh air! It's exactly what you need. What we need.

VOICE. I never thought I'd live so far away from people.

GABE. We're twenty minutes from the city.

VOICE. Growing up, I was like, "As soon as you are out of range of people, you will be taken and no one will ever notice."

GABE. Presumably, Dave and Ruth might've said something.

VOICE. I figured they'd be happy to move on to their next adoptee. To someone better, blonder –

GABE. And less anxious?

VOICE. Or at least less prone to kidnappers.

(VOICE half-gets up.)

You locked the door, right?

GABE. Yes. Now sit down.

(VOICE relents, sits down. They relax.)

You'll feel better once we get stuff of our own. *(re: easy chair)* And we can get rid of this crap.

VOICE. You don't like it?

GABE. Do you?

VOICE. It goes with the living room.

GABE. Yeah, our hideous new living room.

VOICE. You said you liked it.

GABE. I said it is exactly what it should be: a shitty first house. *(beat)* Our shitty first house.

VOICE. Well, I like it. It called to me.

GABE. "It called to you?"

VOICE. Hasn't that ever happened to you?

GABE. No?

VOICE. You see a place and it just says –

(Behind them, a voice from nowhere –)

WALL. HELLO

VOICE. Exactly!

GABE. What?

VOICE. What you said.

GABE. I didn't say anything.

VOICE. Well, I just saw it and I knew. (beat) We should keep the chair. Just in case the old tenants come back for it.

GABE. Chair like this? If they left it, they're not coming back for it.

(Someone's phone rings. VOICE finds GABE's pocket, checks his phone.)

Who is it?

VOICE. Your mom.

GABE. Oh. Weird.

    (**GABE** *answers.*)

    Hey.

    Okay.

    Yeah, put her on.

    Yeah, I'm listening.

    …

    (excited) Wait, WHAT?!

VOICE. What? What?!

GABE. No, yeah! Congratulations!

    Marriage. Big stuff.

VOICE. Big stuff who? Big stuff who?

GABE. *(to* **VOICE***)* It's Jenny.

VOICE. Jenny?

GABE. So how'd he propose?

VOICE. And Steve Scumbag? I thought they broke up.

    (**GABE** *waves* **VOICE** *away from the phone.*)

GABE. *(to phone)* Yeah, uh huh –

    (**GABE** *gestures: "five minutes!" as he exits to the bedroom.*)

VOICE. Okay.

    I've got stuff to do, too, you know!

    Work.

    Awesome work.

    Yep.

    Yes, I do.

    Busy as well.

    Talking to myself.

    (**VOICE** *rolls over, digs into her purse, and pulls out a bound stack of pages. She pulls out a pen, starts editing a safety manual.*)

"To reduce the risk of fire, electrical shock, or – "
(corrects) "INJURY when using YOUR dishwasher,
follow basic precautions including the followING – "

*(Her pen runs out of ink. She looks around for a new
pen. Behind her, a white piece of paper drops down
from the* **WALL**. **VOICE** *notices something falling to the
ground. She picks it up, looks at it. Weird. Where did
this come from? Maybe it's one of her papers.)*

"Hetchman sat alone in easy chair."

(A strange noise from somewhere in the house.)

Gabe?

*(***VOICE*** continues editing.)*

(corrects) "Hetchman sat alone in HIS easy chair."

*(***HETCHMAN*** appears in the living room easy chair. He
wears a hat we saw earlier. This startles* **VOICE** *for a
moment but she continues to read.)*

"Wearing A hat. A well-balanced man'S hat. IT was
perfect."

(This is obviously not a safety manual. Nevertheless,
VOICE *continues.)*

(Focus shifts to **HETCHMAN** *'s world:* **HETCHMAN**
watches TV in the easy chair. His chair. Everything
HETCHMAN *needs is precisely within arm's reach.
Anything not in arm's reach can be gotten with the
assistance of a trash picker-upper.)*

*(***HETCHMAN*** wears the same clothes every day. Or
perhaps variations of the same outfit. And most
importantly, he always wears the same hat.)*

(We watch **HETCHMAN** *watch the TV. He laughs at the
TV, eats another peanut.)*

"Next day-"

(HETCHMAN in the same position. He has a terrible itch in his crotch/thigh region. He considers reaching into his pants to scratch himself. Can anyone see from the window? More importantly, does it matter? He digs into his pants, scratches the itch. Ahh.)

"Next day – "

(HETCHMAN in the same position. He hocks the phlegm in his throat, spits into a tissue. He ineffectually tosses the tissue towards a nearby trashcan. He considers retrieving the tissue, but does not.)

"Next day – "

(HETCHMAN in the same position. Something is not quite right. He reaches up to his head, feels around. He does not feel a hat. Where is his hat?!)

HETCHMAN. Ey. Ey, wife!

HETCHMAN'S WIFE. *(offstage)* What!

HETCHMAN. I said, ey, wife!

(HETCHMAN'S WIFE enters with the laundry.)

HETCHMAN'S WIFE. I said, what?

HETCHMAN. You see my hat?

HETCHMAN'S WIFE. What hat?

HETCHMAN. My hat, I always wear.

HETCHMAN'S WIFE. That old hat? No, I don't see it lately.

HETCHMAN. Whatchu mean you don't see it lately? I wear it every day.

HETCHMAN'S WIFE. You think I look at you every day or something?

HETCHMAN. Whatchu be looking at instead, uh?

HETCHMAN'S WIFE. Maybe you get up, you do a little housework, and maybe THEN you find hat.

HETCHMAN. Is good thinking!

You start first, okay? Okay.

VOICE. "Next day – "

HETCHMAN. You think maybe you wash it?

HETCHMAN'S WIFE. Wash what?

HETCHMAN. My hat.

HETCHMAN'S WIFE. Why I wash a hat for, uh?

VOICE. "Next day – "

HETCHMAN. You look in bedroom?

HETCHMAN'S WIFE. There is no hat in bedroom!

HETCHMAN. You look then?

HETCHMAN'S WIFE. If there is hat in bedroom, I will see it, okay?

HETCHMAN. Okay.

You should look, though. I am thinking maybe it is in there.

VOICE. "Next day – "

HETCHMAN. You see it now?

HETCHMAN'S WIFE. No.

VOICE. "Next day – "

HETCHMAN. How 'bout now?

HETCHMAN'S WIFE. No!

VOICE. "Next day – "

HETCHMAN. You see it now, right?

HETCHMAN'S WIFE. Hetchman: I don't see it today. I don't see it yesterday. I am thinking MAYBE: you lose hat.

HETCHMAN. How I lose hat?

HETCHMAN'S WIFE. Maybe hat it walk away.

HETCHMAN. But hat does not have legs.

HETCHMAN'S WIFE. You want to find hat?

You look for hat. Yourself.

*(***HETCHMAN'S WIFE*** exits.)*

VOICE. "More and more, thoughts of the hat consumed Hetchman.

He changed the channel"

HETCHMAN. – to hat-related program.

VOICE. "He watched a scary movie"

HETCHMAN. – and reach to hat for comfort.

VOICE. "He ate from his canister of nuts"

HETCHMAN. – which feature hat-wearing peanut. Maybe is behind TV?

(Without getting up, **HETCHMAN** *strains to look under the TV.)*

VOICE. "But it was not behind the TV, nor was it in any of the handful of places Hetchman searched. The hat being just the first of two possessions that would go missing in the days that followed."

*(***HETCHMAN'S WIFE** *enters in her coat.)*

HETCHMAN'S WIFE. The Mendelssohns are outside, I think they leave without us.

HETCHMAN. Eh, I don't like the fucking Mendelssohns. I see the Mendelssohns and I want to vomit all over. Why we eat with people like that, uh?

HETCHMAN'S WIFE. You seen this one before.

HETCHMAN. No.

HETCHMAN'S WIFE. "Life After People?" Is rerun!

HETCHMAN. Is ten-part series!

HETCHMAN'S WIFE. Is so boring, I don't know how you watch.

HETCHMAN. Is good show!

Is what world will be like after people they are all dead.

Is fun time!

*(***HETCHMAN'S WIFE** *hears a noise. She looks up.)*

VOICE. "And then all at once, she heard it, low and mournful."

HETCHMAN'S WIFE. You hear that?

HETCHMAN. What?

HETCHMAN'S WIFE. That sound. That, *rumble.*

HETCHMAN. Is fart?

HETCHMAN'S WIFE. Is not fart.

HETCHMAN. Is probably just TV program, is all.

(HETCHMAN'S WIFE *exits, listening.*)

VOICE. "Hetchman failed to notice his wife's apprehension, so consumed he was by his beloved TV program. The more he watched, the more he fantasized about a world empty of people. He imagined his neighbors – "

HETCHMAN. Dead.

VOICE. "His podiatrist – "

HETCHMAN. Dead.

VOICE. "Even the weeds in his lawn, the feral cats his wife chased off from time to time – "

HETCHMAN. Dead dead dead dead dead.

VOICE. "The once great and powerful hatmaker happily mused on the eventual fate of the hatless masses."

(HETCHMAN *chuckles to himself, contented.*)

VOICE. "It would be hours before Hetchman finally looked up and realized – "

HETCHMAN. She is gone?

(*Without leaving his chair,* HETCHMAN *leans back to see if she's in the bedroom. No. He leans further to see if she's in the bathroom. He almost falls over. He catches himself, exhales. Too much exertion.*)

HETCHMAN. (*dismissive*) Eh, she is not gone.

VOICE. "Tomorrow, he thought. Tomorrow, he would look and tomorrow, he would find."

(HETCHMAN *watches the TV, falls asleep.* VOICE *reaches the end of the page.* HETCHMAN *disappears from view.* GABE *enters.*)

GABE. Well, mark your calendar! Memorial Day weekend, coming to a non-denominational chapel-slash-golf resort near you.

VOICE. When did they get back together?

GABE. Couple months ago.

VOICE. But he's Steve Scumbag.

GABE. Well, he's her Steve Scumbag now. Which reminds me, we should probably stop saying that since I kept slipping on the phone just now.

VOICE. What made her change her mind?

GABE. Who knows. *(beat)* According to her, the moment she first knew she loved him, she was recovering from the mono that he gave her. My sister's not big on picking the right time and place for things.

VOICE. Love and disease know no boundaries!

GABE. What about you? What was your moment?

VOICE. Why does there need to be a moment?

GABE. I had a moment.

VOICE. When?

GABE. Our last night in Costa Rica and you lost your shoe and we had to walk all the way back.

VOICE. That was a misfortune, not a moment.

GABE. I felt this little ping in my breast pocket. I thought someone had sent me a text, but it was actually just my heart thinking about you.

VOICE. Wow.

GABE. True.

VOICE. And to think, for me, it was that your douchebag quotient was so much lower compared to everyone else's.

GABE. You mean compared to your previous consecutive boyfriends?

VOICE. You and Jose overlapped by like, the tiniest bit.

GABE. Two weeks.

VOICE. I don't like being single, so what?

GABE. You're like a machine.

(**GABE** *kisses her, starts to exit.*)

VOICE. Where're you going?

GABE. Sleep?

VOICE. This early?

GABE. My first period class starts at seven-fifteen. This is not early.

VOICE. What about the video?

GABE. First thing tomorrow, I promise. The boxes'll be there when we wake up.

(GABE *starts to go off towards the bedroom.*)

VOICE. Don't leave me.

GABE. Sorry, but daybreak waits for no man!

(GABE *knocks against the* **WALL** *for emphasis. In response, the* **WALL** *makes a strange noise. Ow. Only* **VOICE** *hears this.*)

VOICE. What was that?

GABE. What?

VOICE. You didn't hear it?

GABE. *(hushed)* Oh wait, actually, I think I did.

VOICE. Really?

GABE. Yeah. That is the sound of your brain ticking. That is the reason you can never fall asleep.

VOICE. That's not true. I sleep.

GABE. Then you get up, do laps around the living room, make yourself a bowl of oatmeal, and go BACK to sleep at four in the morning. I'm surprised your roommates never said anything.

VOICE. How do you know that? You don't know that.

(GABE *makes a little "BOOM! Revelation!" noise/ gesture.*)

GABE. That's why this'll be good. *(beat)* See? I know you. You don't think I know you, but I do. I see everything.

VOICE. Not everything.

GABE. I'm a motherfucking knowledge ninja.

(GABE *ninjas out of the room.* **VOICE** *considers taking the* **WALL** *papers with her, but under* GABE*'s gaze, she does not. She instead looks around the room one last time and turns off the lights. She follows* GABE *into the bedroom.*)

Scene

(Next morning)

*(**VOICE** gets ready to take a video, sets up the living room just so. The **WALL** sends down a paper. **VOICE** sees a flash of white as it falls to the ground. She looks for it.)*

*(As she searches, getting closer, the **WALL** says, not too loudly –)*

WALL. UH HUH

UH HUH

*(**VOICE** finds the paper.)*

BINGO

*(**VOICE** definitely hears this. But where is it coming from?)*

VOICE. Hello…?

WALL. HELLO

*(Okay, that came from the **WALL**. **VOICE** approaches the **WALL**.)*

YOU HEAR ME?

VOICE. *(small)* Yes?

WALL. I HEAR YOU

*(**VOICE** drops her camera.)*

VOICE. Omigod! Gabe. GABE!

WALL. WAIT!

*(**GABE** enters in work clothes. Probably a shirt and tie.)*

GABE. What?! What?!

VOICE. The wall.

GABE. What about the wall?

VOICE. Listen.

*(**GABE** puts an ear to the **WALL**.)*

GABE. Okay.

WALL. HEY THERE, HOT STUFF

VOICE. There!

GABE. What?

VOICE. You didn't hear that?

>   (**GABE** *listens harder.*)

GABE. You mean the radiator?

VOICE. No.

>   (**GABE** *peeks out the window.*)

GABE. Could be the neighbors.

VOICE. It's not the neighbors.

GABE. My parents used to have cats underneath their porch. They sound just like babies.

VOICE. It wasn't a cat.

GABE. Then what was it?

VOICE. I…don't actually know.

GABE. So are we doing this?

VOICE. Huh?

GABE. The video? I got my good tie on for this, you know. *(waits)* Or we can just not, I guess.

>   (**VOICE** *doesn't move, still staring at the* **WALL**.*)

GABE. You okay?

VOICE. Yeah. I'm fine. I think I'll just skip work today.

GABE. You feeling sick?

VOICE. No. I just feel like taking a break, is all.

GABE. Little Miss Perfect, taking a break! That's new.

VOICE. New home, new priorities.

GABE. Well! I gotta go. Some of the kids are coming in early to set up their presentations. Call me if you need anything.

VOICE. Okay.

GABE. See you.

>   (**GABE** *kisses* **VOICE**, *exits. Beat.*)

VOICE. What is this?

WALL. EH?

VOICE. What are you?

WALL. ME?
> I AM WALL. I AM WALL OF TRUTH
> WHICH MAKE ME
> SO AWESOME SO AWESOME SO AWESOME
> (YAY)

VOICE. Oh boy.

WALL. MAYBE YOU WONDER
> WHAT IS WALL?
> WHY IS WALL HERE?
> IS WALL A HE?
> MAYBE IS WOMAN
> WHO KNOWS!
> WALL KNOW
> BECAUSE WALL KNOW ALL

VOICE. Okay then why doesn't he hear you?

WALL. YOU MEAN HOT STUFF?

VOICE. Yes.

WALL. IF YOU HEAR WALL, YOU MUST BE SPECIAL TYPE PERSON
> IS NOT EVERY DAY SOMEONE THEY HEAR WALL.

VOICE. I am a copy editor. Of safety manuals.

I am about as unspecial as they come.

So what're you doing in my living room?

WALL. WALL IS EVERYWHERE
> YOU ARE IN BED?
> YOU ARE ON TOILET?
> I SEE ALL
> (I CLOSE MY EYES IF YOU ARE ON TOILET, THOUGH)
> (I AM RESPECTFUL WALL)
> I AM MOST IMPORTANT CHARACTER IN STORY

VOICE. Wait, "story?"

WALL. YES: STORY.

VOICE. What story are you referring to?

(The **WALL** *sends down a paper.)*

VOICE. This is your story? The hat guy?

WALL. FOR SURE

VOICE. Just one more page, okay?

WALL. OKAY!

*(***VOICE*** begins to read the paper.* **HETCHMAN** *appears again in his chair.* **VOICE** *picks up the paper.)*

VOICE. "Hetchman's thoughts remained so muddled by the disappearance of his hat, that even when his best friend and next door neighbor Meckel entered, Hetchman could only hear – "

*(***MECKEL*** enters in a perfectly* **MECKEL***-like hat.)*

MECKEL. Hat hat hat? Hat hat hat. Hatman. Hatman.

HETCHMAN. Uh?

*(***MECKEL*** nudges* **HETCHMAN***.)*

MECKEL. Hetchman. Hetchman.

HETCHMAN. Oh. Ey, Meckel.

*(***MECKEL*** looks at* **HETCHMAN***. Something is different.)*

MECKEL. You get haircut?

HETCHMAN. No.

MECKEL. You get sunburn?

HETCHMAN. No.

MECKEL. You sure? 'Cause there is something different about you –

HETCHMAN. My hat!

MECKEL. Oh yeah.

HETCHMAN. Is gone!

MECKEL. Is gone?!

HETCHMAN. Is poofed!

MECKEL. Is poofed?!

HETCHMAN. My hat, is – is –

*(**HETCHMAN** hyperventilates. **MECKEL** grabs **HETCHMAN**.)*

MECKEL. Ey, Hetchman. Hetchman – !

Is okay, okay?

*(**HETCHMAN** breathes.)*

HETCHMAN. Okay.

MECKEL. Is probably just below chair.

HETCHMAN. Is below chair?

MECKEL. Or somewhere. Is probably just –

*(**MECKEL** stifles a laugh.)*

HETCHMAN. What.

MECKEL. Is nothing, is just – you sure look strange without hat. I never notice, your head, how it is –

*(**MECKEL** makes a noise that suggests how weird **HETCHMAN**'s head is without his hat.)*

MECKEL. Anyway. You ask your wife? Where is she?

HETCHMAN. Who?

MECKEL. Wife.

HETCHMAN. MY wife?

MECKEL. Yeah.

(As if realizing it for the first time...)

HETCHMAN. Oh, I don't know.

MECKEL. She is gone, too?

HETCHMAN. Eh, she is probably doing shitwork, or being chased by small dog.

*(**MECKEL** looks around, peeks into the bedroom.)*

MECKEL. Her purse, it is gone.

HETCHMAN. Oh yeah?

MECKEL. So she is missing, too.

HETCHMAN. Okay.

MECKEL. And you sit here, all alone, no one to love you?

HETCHMAN. I watch TV program, is okay.

MECKEL. Next time, you call my house, I come over right away.

HETCHMAN. Eh.

(**MECKEL** *adjusts his hat, stretches.*)

MECKEL. Okay. I love you.

HETCHMAN. What.

MECKEL. You come into my arms, I love you a little.

HETCHMAN. I do not need loving!

MECKEL. You are looking a little floaty. Is okay, I do it real fast, is like two seconds.

(**MECKEL** *forces himself on* **HETCHMAN**. *Mmm, hug.*)

HETCHMAN. Enough! Enough! Meckel! Getgetget!

(**MECKEL** *gently releases* **HETCHMAN**.)

MECKEL. Ohhhhh.

See? You look so much better.

Okay: now I help you find wife.

HETCHMAN. I am not looking for wife.

I am looking for hat.

MECKEL. Okay, but –

Hat and wife, they disappear same time?

HETCHMAN. Yeah?

MECKEL. Then maybe you find wife: you find hat.

(**MECKEL** *lets this sink in.* **HETCHMAN** *is suddenly more attentive in his own lazy way.*)

HETCHMAN. Ohh.

MECKEL. Maybe wife leave because you and wife, you fight?

HETCHMAN. We do not fight.

MECKEL. No?

HETCHMAN. How can we fight? We don't even talk!

MECKEL. Or maybe she say something important before she go?

HETCHMAN. Hat?

MECKEL. Wife.

HETCHMAN. Oh. No.

MECKEL. Maybe she say something like – ?

(**HETCHMAN'S WIFE** *appears.*)

HETCHMAN'S WIFE. I wash dishes

I want hat

I go to store

I want hat

I make the mandelbread

I want hat

I want hat

HETCHMAN. She want cat…?

HETCHMAN'S WIFE. I want *hat*!

(**HETCHMAN'S WIFE** *disappears.*)

HETCHMAN. Or maybe she get lost in field, I don't know!

MECKEL. You know what you do?

You call her name.

HETCHMAN. What?

MECKEL. Then she will have to come back.

With hat!

HETCHMAN. Oh yeah. Is good thinking, Meckel!

MECKEL. Okay?

HETCHMAN. Okay!

MECKEL. You know her name, right?

HETCHMAN. Is my wife!

MECKEL. Okay: and go!

(waits) You start any time now.

HETCHMAN. Or Meckel, maybe you say it for me.

You have loud voice, everyone they will hear.

MECKEL. You don't know her name?

HETCHMAN. I know her name!

MECKEL. Okay. Then you just say, "Ey!… Name!" Okay?

HETCHMAN. Okay. Ey – !

(**HETCHMAN** *opens his mouth. He waits for her name to come to him. Wait a minute, what is her name?*)

HETCHMAN. … [mumbles name].

MECKEL. You don't know her name?

HETCHMAN. Has been long time since I call to her.

And you don't know either!

MECKEL. Is not my wife!

HETCHMAN. So?

MECKEL. Maybe wall know.

HETCHMAN. *(aside)* Eh! Don't ask wall. Wall is big stupid.

MECKEL. Ey, wall! Whatsherface, you know her name?

WALL. NOT A CLUE

SORRY, MECKEL.

MECKEL. Is okay!

HETCHMAN. See? Big stupid!

MECKEL. Or maybe, you write her letter.

HETCHMAN. Uh?

MECKEL. Maybe you woo her with a "I love you" letter.

HETCHMAN. But we are not the "I love you" type.

We are more of the "I guess I am married to you so oh well" type.

MECKEL. Write letter: and mail will find her.

HETCHMAN. Yeah, maybe I write letter –

(**HETCHMAN** *starts watching TV.*)

HETCHMAN. – right after TV program it end.

MECKEL. Hetchman, c'mon, you need to –

(**MECKEL** *is also dazzled by the TV. They temporarily abandon their search.*)

Scene

(The train)

VOICE. "And as Hetchman and Meckel were temporarily dazzled by the TV, Hetchman's Wife found herself – for the first time in her life – alone, awake, and on the train."

*(*HETCHMAN'S WIFE* sits next to the hat on the train. This is* HETCHMAN*'s hat. She tries to look out the window, but can't concentrate.)*

*(*HETCHMAN'S WIFE* picks up the hat, places it on her head. She waits. Nothing. She tosses the hat aside.)*

HETCHMAN'S WIFE. I used to hate you.

I used to dream about the day he would lose you

On sailboat

In blizzard.

And I would be such a good wife.

But every day he come home, he come home with you.

How you feel now, now he is not here to protect you, uh?

*(*HETCHMAN'S WIFE* pokes the hat.)*

HETCHMAN'S WIFE. Is lucky I need you.

Otherwise, hat you would not be so safe.

Whatchu think of that, uh?

Uh?

You have nothing to say?

(The hat says nothing.)

Scene

(Living room)

(VOICE *continues reading as* **GABE** *enters with takeout.)*

GABE. Hey.

VOICE. Hey.

*(***GABE** *takes in the mess of papers around* **VOICE.***)*

GABE. Am I interrupting?

VOICE. No.

GABE. What happened to your break?

VOICE. They said it was urgent.

GABE. You work on safety manuals. When is it ever urgent?

VOICE. I promised I'd look at it.

GABE. I thought we did this so you could get away from it all.

VOICE. We did this 'cause my roommate got married and my lease was up.

GABE. Technically, yes. But getting away from the work should be a side perk.

VOICE. I can get away from work. I can get away whenever I want.

GABE. So that…?

VOICE. …is work that I can do later.

*(***GABE** *looks at* **VOICE'***s papers. She puts them down.)*

VOICE. That I will do later.

GABE. Good. 'Cause I got Indian. Your favorite.

VOICE. Aw, thanks.

GABE. Also: next Friday, we're getting dinner. The whole family. For Jenny and Steve.

VOICE. Okay.

GABE. As in you're invited.

VOICE. Me?

GABE. Family, that's you basically.

VOICE. I don't know. You guys like to do your thing together.

GABE. You mean eat?

VOICE. You know what I mean.

GABE. And Steve Scumbag's still working for that publishing house.

VOICE. So?

GABE. You want to do what he does. So ask him. Perfect opportunity.

VOICE. Yeah, but I have no experience in that.

GABE. That's kind of the point.

VOICE. But to get where he's at, I'd have to do another seven years of intern entry-level crap that I don't think I'm prepared for. And I'm six months away from a promotion. Once I get that, it'll be so much better.

GABE. Or you can just quit.

(VOICE *accidentally knocks into something. It's* HETCHMAN*'s peanut canister. She shrugs, opens it, eats the remaining peanuts inside.*)

VOICE. Quitting is not part of the plan.

GABE. Not everything has to be a plan. And I think you'd be fantastic at whatever it is you want to do.

VOICE. I'll come to dinner. And I'll sit next to him.

GABE. Good. *(re: peanuts)* Now stop that. We're eating.

(GABE *opens up the takeout,* VOICE *joins him. She looks back at her pages longingly. She almost reaches out to them, before* GABE *catches her.*)

Scene

(Living room)

(VOICE *finishes the remnants of the takeout. She looks around for* **GABE.** *)*

VOICE. Is he asleep?

WALL. COAST IT IS CLEAR

(VOICE *picks up a page.)*

VOICE. Finally.

WALL. YOU DON'T WANT HIM, WALL CAN TAKE HIM

VOICE. Really? 'Cause I'd love to see you try.

WALL. EY

WALL CAN MAKE THINGS HAPPEN
YOU WILL SEE

VOICE. Ha. "And back at home, Hetchman wrote a letter – "

WALL. TO HIS MISSING LOVE

(HETCHMAN *still in his chair. He now has a firefighter hat on his head. The living room is just a bit messier and smellier, just as he is just a bit messier and smellier than last time.)*

HETCHMAN. Who you talking to, wall?

WALL. NO ONE

NO ONE YOU KNOW
YET

HETCHMAN. Oh okay.

(HETCHMAN *takes out a pen and paper from his pocket. He writes.)*

HETCHMAN. Dear…hat.

If you are reading this, ey, you can read!

Awesome job, hat.

Is very cool thing you know how to read.

Also, kudos to mail service for finding you even when I cannot.

Tax dollars at work: totally cool!

How are you, hat?

Are you happy?

Are you lost?

Have you grown legs which you use to run away from me?

I wish you had a name, hat

So I could call to you

And you would have to come back to me

Which would be totally easier.

But you are hat, and so you do not

Which is big bummer.

I miss you.

Your Hetchman.

(*Then as a post-script – *)

HETCHMAN. And if you see wife, you tell her floor it is full of the dust bunny, so maybe when she come back, she clean it?

(**HETCHMAN** *finishes his letter. He holds the letter up in the air, waits, looks around.*)

HETCHMAN. Ey, wife!

WALL. SHE IS NOT HERE

HETCHMAN. Oh right. Thanks, wall.

WALL. NO PROBLEMO

HETCHMAN. Maybe you mail letter for me?

WALL. I AM WALL.

HETCHMAN. Oh. Right. Okay, I get mailman do it later.

(**HETCHMAN** *puts the letter away. He reaches into his peanut canister. It's empty.*)

(**HETCHMAN** *sees a new canister of peanuts in arm's reach. He uses his trash picker-upper to retrieve it. He stretches. As soon as he picks it up, it falls out of the picker-upper, rolls away from him. No!*)

(**HETCHMAN** *considers getting up, but doesn't. He turns back to the items around his chair, searches for something, anything to munch on. He finds a bag of cheetos. He doesn't like cheetos, but hey, peanuts would require getting up. So he eats the cheetos, first grudgingly and then more normally.*)

HETCHMAN. Is Elna?

Is Hortza?

Is Wife?

(*Nothing.* **HETCHMAN** *gives up, sighs.*)

VOICE. " – but try as he might, Hetchman simply could not recall the name of the seemingly nameless woman who had spent the past sixty years cooking, cleaning, and loving him to the ground."

Scene

(Living room)

(VOICE puts down her piece of paper.)

VOICE. I don't get it.

WALL. EH?

VOICE. "Loving him to the ground?"

WALL. OH

WELL

FOR YOU, I EXPLAIN

(Lights up on MECKEL, who explains.)

MECKEL. Okay, so:

"Love keep you grounded."

Is true!

(Lights up on an example: a baby in a pink blanket, maybe attached to a bunch of balloons. MECKEL holds the baby from floating away.)

MECKEL. From the moment you are born, baby, she need love.

Otherwise, she float off into the sky like balloon.

(MECKEL lets go of the baby, it begins to float up.)

MECKEL. I love you!

(The baby sinks down for a moment, then rises back up.)

MECKEL. I love you!

(Baby sinks, then rises.)

MECKEL. I...*don't* love you!

(Baby continues to rise, but MECKEL holds it down.)

MECKEL. And then she become loveless lonesome her whole life.

Is big bummer!

But baby is small and easy to love, so she usually stay on ground.

The longer you live, the more love you need.

The more love you have, the longer you live.

WALL. IS WHY MECKEL WILL LIVE FOREVER

(**MECKEL** *blushes.*)

MECKEL. Oh well –

WALL. IS TRUE

MECKEL. Is mostly true.

Because even though my wife, she is long dead from seagull attack, I am having plenty of small ones to love me, so is okay.

WALL. EVERYONE'S FAVORITE GRANDPA MECKEL. EVERYONE'S BEST HELPER MECKEL. EVERYONE'S SECRET SMOOCHER MECKEL.

(*Awkward pause.* **MECKEL** *tries to ignore this last statement.*)

MECKEL. Is why parents they nag, "You find girlfriend yet?"

'Cause if you are late bloomer, they have to love you extra long time, which is huge pain in the ass to do.

Is also why parents they are eager for the grandchildren.

Is like, "I am feeling a little floaty today, you have baby yet?"

"I don't stay here so long you don't have small one soon!"

(**MECKEL** *puts a clothespin on his nose.*)

And is why I go hug increasingly stinky pal Hetchman.

Because I am and have always been loyal friend, cool protector Meckel.

Because once you become floaty, this feeling you will never lose.

And forever after –

MECKEL/VOICE. " – wherever you are, whoever you're with, something will always be not quite right."

(MECKEL *disappears.* VOICE *folds up the paper.*)

WALL. EH?

VOICE. What.

WALL. THAT FEELING, YOU KNOW IT?

VOICE. Sure, sometimes.

WALL. EVEN WITH HOT STUFF?

VOICE. With anyone, I guess. I'm just not the kind of person who gets all emotional about things. That's all.

(VOICE *clears her throat. New topic.*)

VOICE. Next page?

(*The* WALL *sends down another paper.*)

VOICE. Thank you.

WALL. UH HUH

VOICE. "At the hatmaker's shop – "

WALL. IN WHICH WALL PLAY HATMAKER FOR DRAMATIC EFFECT

(*The wall clears its throat.*)

Scene

(The hatmaker's shop)

(**HETCHMAN'S WIFE** *stands nervously at the hatmaker's counter in a shop three towns over. The wall perhaps wears a moustache and hat for disguise.*)

HETCHMAN'S WIFE. They tell me you make hat.

WALL. YOU WANT HAT?

(**HETCHMAN'S WIFE** *produces* **HETCHMAN** *'s hat.*)

HETCHMAN'S WIFE. I want this hat.

You make copy for me?

(The **HATMAKER** *examines the hat.)*

WALL. SO WHAT?
YOU THINK YOU HAVE HAT
YOU WILL HEAR THE HATMUSIC?

HETCHMAN'S WIFE. Is just hat, is all – !

WALL. IS NO HATMUSIC FOR THE WOMAN
IS JUST NOT POSSIBLE

HETCHMAN'S WIFE. But they tell me you are second-best hatmaker around.

So surely you make it for me, uh?

WALL. AND HETCHMAN, HE CANNOT MAKE HAT FOR YOU?

HETCHMAN'S WIFE. Hetchman he does not believe in hat for me.

I want hat

And Hetchman he say –

(Flashback to **HETCHMAN** *in his chair, eating peanuts.)*

HETCHMAN. No good!

So silly!

Hat?! For lady?!

(**HETCHMAN** *nearly dies of laughing, chokes on a peanut.*)

HETCHMAN'S WIFE. So all this time, I never have hat.

Is like everything else I have wanted.

I want flower

And Hetchman he say –

(**HETCHMAN** *eats a fruit cup.*)

HETCHMAN. Flower?!

HETCHMAN'S WIFE. You buy flower for Autzel the shoemaker's wife.

HETCHMAN. Autzel's wife, she die of unfortunate foot fungus!

I have to buy flower for fucking dead woman, is rule!

HETCHMAN'S WIFE. I want passion

And Hetchman he say –

HETCHMAN. Why I need to show you passion, uh?

HETCHMAN'S WIFE. Meckel feels passion for Doshka.

HETCHMAN. Doshka is slightly stupid dead woman!

Passion for dead woman is like passion for trashcan, is easy!

Here. I give you rest of fruit cocktail.

(**HETCHMAN** *offers a spoonful of fruit, gestures for an "aaah" from his* **WIFE.**)

HETCHMAN. Is good as passion. Is passionfruit!

HETCHMAN'S WIFE. I want baby

And Hetchman he say –

(*We wait for* **HETCHMAN** *to speak. He doesn't hear her. Or maybe he does and just ignores her?*)

HETCHMAN'S WIFE. And Hetchman he say nothing.

(**HETCHMAN** *disappears out of the scene.*)

HETCHMAN'S WIFE. So I don't ask Hetchman anymore.

Now I ask myself

And me? I say okay!

WALL. I CANNOT MAKE HAT LIKE THIS
IS ONLY ONE WHO CAN MAKE HAT LIKE THIS
AND YOU ARE HIS WIFE

(The sound of a distant rumbling. **HETCHMAN'S WIFE**
is alarmed by this noise. She grabs the hat.)

HETCHMAN'S WIFE. I will find someone else.

I will go to third-best hatmaker and he will make hat
for me.

*(***HETCHMAN'S WIFE*** *hurries off with the hat.)*

WALL. IS USELESS!
YOU WILL FAIL

(The wall turns to us.)

WALL. WOMEN: IS SO CRAZY, UH?

Scene

(Living room)

VOICE. "And several nights later, while Hetchman dreamed of hats, his living room found itself the place of an unexpected conspiracy – "

(MECKEL on the phone in HETCHMAN's living room, as HETCHMAN snores softly. On the other end is HETCHMAN'S WIFE on a pay phone.)

MECKEL. You still have hat?

HETCHMAN'S WIFE. I still have hat.

But third-best hatmaker he say no.

So now I go to fourth-best hatmaker and I get him to make me hat!

MECKEL. Or maybe you come home.

Since Hetchman he miss you so much.

HETCHMAN'S WIFE. Oh really.

MECKEL. Oh yeah. Like potato chip!

HETCHMAN'S WIFE. You sure? 'Cause mail drop off letter. Hetchman he write a letter to a stupid hat!

MECKEL. Mail service is amazing, uh? Is always getting to the right person!

HETCHMAN'S WIFE. So you don't have to lie to me, Meckel.

MECKEL. Even when is lie for good cause? *(beat)* Really, though, he is falling apart without you.

HETCHMAN'S WIFE. He is stinking?

MECKEL. He is smelling so bad!

HETCHMAN'S WIFE. Is dirty?

MECKEL. Is pigsty!

HETCHMAN'S WIFE. Is awful?

MECKEL. Is disgusting!

(HETCHMAN'S WIFE smiles to herself.)

MECKEL. I am having to wear clothespin even to say brief hi.

Is why I miss you.

HETCHMAN'S WIFE. Thank you, Meckel.

MECKEL. And he has been like floaty baby without hat.

You know how his head is like –

*(**MECKEL** and **HETCHMAN'S WIFE** both make sounds to describe how **HETCHMAN**'s head looks. They laugh.)*

HETCHMAN'S WIFE. Is true.

MECKEL. He kind of deserve it, though. To not have hat.

But maybe I can tell him, hat is okay?

HETCHMAN'S WIFE. Meckel.

MECKEL. Is not right to keep secret from Hetchman.

Is making me wish you had not called me so I would not know.

You tell me to ask him for your name, and I don't think he has it.

HETCHMAN'S WIFE. What?!

MECKEL. I am thinking he has forgotten your name.

HETCHMAN'S WIFE. So I have lost name.

MECKEL. You don't say a name for so long, is easy to forget.

HETCHMAN'S WIFE. Doshka always had her name.

MECKEL. Is Doshka! Is easy.

Because me, I am lousy with the names.

HETCHMAN'S WIFE. I remember when you last said my name.

MECKEL. Oh? I don't remember.

HETCHMAN'S WIFE. Yes, you do. Was twenty years ago.

*(Flashback to **HETCHMAN'S WIFE** who has been crying. She folds up a pink blanket. **MECKEL** enters, stops.)*

MECKEL. Is bad time?

HETCHMAN'S WIFE. No.

MECKEL. Hetchman, he is at work?

I can go.

HETCHMAN'S WIFE. No, is okay.

How is Doshka? She is thinking girl or boy?

MECKEL. Another girl.

HETCHMAN'S WIFE. Another girl!

Is good!

Is good to have multiple girl and multiple boy.

MECKEL. Is probably last one anyway.

… I mean, is not too late to have small one. Is just Doshka and me, we have enough small ones to field whole potato race team!

HETCHMAN'S WIFE. Yeah.

MECKEL. Is good you are strong wife.

I am thinking you are strongest wife I know

And is not just because you win husband-lifting relay three times running.

HETCHMAN'S WIFE. You think so?

MECKEL. Yeah!

Sometimes I think maybe I should not have married slightly stupid, sexy-looking wife.

Sometimes I think I should have married strong, smart, same-thinking wife.

Like you

(corrects) Like Hetchman and you.

You know,

Like that.

(an awkward pause)

HETCHMAN'S WIFE. But Doshka she choose you. So she cannot be so stupid.

MECKEL. No.

Only slightly!

Is good you will always be Hetchman's Wife.

Is good thing to be wife of hatmaker, you know?

HETCHMAN'S WIFE. *(sadly)* I know.

MECKEL. Ey! Is okay, okay?

*(***MECKEL*** *opens his arms, friendly.* **HETCHMAN'S WIFE** *hugs him with increasing desperation.* **MECKEL** *waits. Finally, she releases him.)*

HETCHMAN'S WIFE. Sorry.

MECKEL. Is okay.

HETCHMAN'S WIFE. You were looking a little floaty, is all.

MECKEL. Oh.

Oh yeah!

HETCHMAN'S WIFE. Hetchman, I don't know if he will be home soon.

Maybe you go back to Doshka.

MECKEL. Okay.

*(***MECKEL*** *and* **HETCHMAN'S WIFE** *hug goodbye. Then snuggle goodbye. Then smooch goodbye. Oops. They separate.)*

HETCHMAN'S WIFE. You go now. Okay, Meckel?

MECKEL. Okay, [name].

(back to the present)

HETCHMAN'S WIFE. Was last time you said my name. Because every time after, I see you, you just look right through me and only call me –

HETCHMAN'S WIFE/MECKEL. Hetchman's Wife.

(The sound of rumbling. **HETCHMAN'S WIFE** *looks back.)*

HETCHMAN'S WIFE. I call you later.

MECKEL. What?!

*(***HETCHMAN'S WIFE*** *hurriedly hangs up.)*

MECKEL. And then you will come home?

And then you will come home?

Whatsyourface?

Whatsyourface!

Hat?

Hat!

(No one responds. **MECKEL** *hangs up.)*

Scene

(Living room)

*(***VOICE*** *finishes with the paper and adds it to an increasingly thick pile.)*

VOICE. So they just forgot her name.

WALL. IS DIFFICULT TO KEEP NAME WHEN NO ONE SAY IT FOR SO LONG

VOICE. Why didn't she leave sooner?

WALL. YOU ARE WIFE

　　YOU ARE HUSBAND

　　YOU HAVE WIFE OR HUSBAND ROLE

　　IS HARD TO SEE DIFFERENT LIFE, IS ALL

VOICE. But at least she gets a hat, right?

WALL. ALL IN DUE TIME, SMALL ONE

　　WALL TELL YOU WHAT HAPPEN HERE LONG TIME AGO

VOICE. Here? They lived here?

WALL. UH HUH

　　IS HETCHMAN FAMILY HOME

　　I AM HETCHMAN FAMILY WALL. I KNOW ALL

VOICE. So what's her name?

WALL. EH?

VOICE. If you know everything.

(The wall dithers.)

WALL. WALL TELL YOU LATER

　　OKAY?

　　OKAY!

　　NEXT PAGE

VOICE. "And late that night, after Meckel tiptoed out of Hetchman's home and back into his own cozy abode, the ground outside of Hetchman's door began to shake – "

(The ground begins to shake. The rumbling sound from earlier is now louder, more present.)

VOICE. "An inhuman voice hit the air. The voice of the golem." *(stops)* Golem? *(reads)* "But for the big stupid among us – " Gee, thanks. "For the big stupid among us who are ignorant of supercool golem ways, a golem is a creature of muck and mud who is sent to our world for many different human purposes. See: 'shoemaker golem' or 'moneyfinder golem.'"

(Lights up on a patch of ground. The ground opens. Something made of mud is lifted out: a GOLEM. The GOLEM yawns, stretches, grows, scratches itself. The mud stiffens into hard dirt as the GOLEM forms.)

VOICE. "The golem rose out of the ground, and Hetchman soon found himself with an unexpected visitor."

(Lights up on HETCHMAN asleep in his easy chair. Suddenly, the GOLEM is behind him. HETCHMAN yawns, looks at the GOLEM, scratches himself, stops. What the fuck, a GOLEM?)

(HETCHMAN shrinks into his chair, hoping the GOLEM will not notice him. The GOLEM smells HETCHMAN, eats a cheeto off of him. HETCHMAN winces as spit dribbles onto his head. If only he had his hat.)

VOICE. "Hetchman would later claim ignorance of the golem's intentions, unaware of the ways in which the monster would forever upend his well-established routine, but the discovery of the power of – "

(Fastforward to HETCHMAN with the bag of cheetos. He tries to control/train the GOLEM.)

HETCHMAN. Cheeto!

(HETCHMAN feeds the GOLEM a cheeto. The GOLEM is excited.)

VOICE. " – helped to keep the unruly golem at bay, though it remained to be seen what kind of golem this golem was."

HETCHMAN. Is cheeto for you.

Is cheeto for me.

(**HETCHMAN** *feeds the* **GOLEM** *another cheeto. The* **GOLEM** *nibbles on the cheeto and* **HETCHMAN**'s *hand, too.*)

HETCHMAN. Ey! Ey now!

(**HETCHMAN** *finds his water spritzer. Throughout the scene,* **HETCHMAN** *alternatively feeds cheetos/threatens to squirt the* **GOLEM**.)

(**HETCHMAN** *feeds the* **GOLEM**. *The* **GOLEM**, *in return, feeds* **HETCHMAN**.)

HETCHMAN. Why thank you!

(**HETCHMAN** *pulls out one last cheeto.* **HETCHMAN** *and the* **GOLEM** *both consider it.*)

HETCHMAN. Is last cheeto.

I am big fan of cheeto.

(*Both wait, then finally –*)

HETCHMAN. Okay, golem, you eat last cheeto.

(*The* **GOLEM** *eats the cheeto right out of* **HETCHMAN**'s *hand, then devours the bag.*)

(*The* **GOLEM** *suddenly smells something. He begins to search around the room, excited.*)

HETCHMAN. Hat? Hat. You find hat for me?

(*The* **GOLEM** *descends into the basement.*)

HETCHMAN. Golem? Ey, golem! You see hat back there?

(*The* **GOLEM** *re-eneters with something.*)

HETCHMAN. Whatchu got there, uh?

(*The* **GOLEM** *holds up a jar, sniffs it.*)

HETCHMAN. You lemme see, and me, I will make you something even better than jar, okay?

(**HETCHMAN** *gets his hands on the jar.*)

HETCHMAN. Okay.

(**HETCHMAN** *examines the jar. It glows pink. He recognizes it.*)

HETCHMAN. Oh.

VOICE. "But rather than listen to the strangely familiar jar now, the retired hatmaker put it aside and instead unlocked the door to his workshop for the first time in many years."

Scene

(Living room)

*(**GABE** enters.)*

GABE. Hey.

VOICE. Hey.

GABE. We missed you.

VOICE. What?

GABE. At dinner?

VOICE. That was tonight?

GABE. I called you.

VOICE. Sorry. I totally blanked.

*(**GABE** is silent.)*

VOICE. Were Jenny and Steve that upset?

GABE. It doesn't matter what they thought.

VOICE. Come on, it couldn't've been that weird without me.

GABE. No, dinner was fine. In fact, it was nice being around people who actually talked to me.

VOICE. I've just been busy with work.

GABE. *(re: papers)* That work?

VOICE. Uh huh.

GABE. That's not work.

VOICE. What do you mean?

GABE. All of a sudden, you have a ton of extra work?

VOICE. So it's not exactly work work. It's still important.

GABE. To who?

VOICE. Me.

GABE. Can you tell me what it is at least?

If it's not work work but it's something important, something you haven't put down since we moved here.

VOICE. You wouldn't understand.

GABE. You haven't even shown me, how can you say I'm not going to understand? Here –

(**GABE** *reaches for the wall papers.* **VOICE** *blocks him. Overlapping...*)

VOICE. Gabe, no.

Gabe, those're mine.

Those're –

GABE. Let me see.

Let me see.

Just let me see!

(**VOICE** *wins. What just happened was strangely intense.*)

VOICE. I'm sorry I missed your dinner, but just let me have this and leave me alone, okay? Okay.

(**GABE** *exits. Back to* **HETCHMAN***'s world. A pile of old things has collected in the living room.*)

VOICE. "For hours, Hetchman worked, fixated on his goal, his hands more nimble and dexterous than they'd been in years, until finally he emerged – "

(**HETCHMAN** *enters with something behind his back.*)

HETCHMAN. Ey, golem. I have surprise for you.

(*The offstange* **GOLEM** *moans: "who, me?"*)

HETCHMAN. Yeah, you. Come on.

(*The* **GOLEM** *crawls out of the basement.*)

HETCHMAN. Close your eyes, okay?

(*The* **GOLEM** *moans: "okay."*)

HETCHMAN. No peeking!

(*The* **GOLEM** *grudgingly closes its eyes.* **HETCHMAN** *drops a hat into the* **GOLEM***'s hands.*)

HETCHMAN. Now open!

(*The* **GOLEM** *opens its eyes. What is this? Food?*)

HETCHMAN. Is hat!

Is hat for wearing.

*(***HETCHMAN*** gestures. The* **GOLEM** *tries on the hat.)*

HETCHMAN. You hear anything?

Any hatmusic?

(The **GOLEM** *concentrates. Maybe a kind of tuba farting noise. The* **GOLEM** *shrugs: "no.")*

HETCHMAN. Is okay. Maybe you hear it later.

But when you are so totally happy

You will hear hatmusic.

Is the most beautiful thing in the world.

(The **GOLEM** *embraces* **HETCHMAN**. **HETCHMAN** *feels something cold and suffocating about the hug. The* **GOLEM** *releases* **HETCHMAN**, *who wheezes.)*

HETCHMAN. Is okay, is just – ooohf!

*(***HETCHMAN*** catches his breath. The* **GOLEM** *tries to hand the hat back to* **HETCHMAN***)*

HETCHMAN. No! Is yours.

You only get one, so don't lose it, okay?

(The **GOLEM** *moans: "okay" and carefully puts the hat aside, descends back into the basement.)*

*(***MECKEL*** enters with a clothespin on his nose, a flashlight in his hand, and a picnic basket of goodies on his arm.)*

MECKEL. Ey, Hetchman, you call for me?

*(***MECKEL*** does a double take:* **HETCHMAN** *is standing?)*

HETCHMAN. Meckel!

*(***HETCHMAN*** hugs* **MECKEL** *a little too long.)*

HETCHMAN. Ohhhh.

*(***MECKEL*** is kind of weirded out by this. He takes off the clothespin.)*

MECKEL. Is good smelling in here.

HETCHMAN. Oh yeah? Must be clean fresh golem scent.

MECKEL. What golem scent?

HETCHMAN. From my new golem!

(The **GOLEM** *pops its head out with a pair of binoculars, waves/moans back.)*

MECKEL. You sure is yours?

HETCHMAN. Is mine! Is a golem of my own!

At first, I thought was trasheater golem, but was actually cool stufffinder golem!

MECKEL. How you know is stufffinder golem?

HETCHMAN. Is all my lost crap.

Is my watch!

Is my old boot!

Look!

Golem, he even find my back!

MECKEL. Your what?

*(**HETCHMAN** stretches for emphasis.)*

HETCHMAN. My back! It went out long time ago and never came back.

Was actually in basement all along!

Was huge pain in the ass not to have.

*(**HETCHMAN** revels in the use of his back. **MECKEL** looks at the **GOLEM**, the **GOLEM** stares down **MECKEL** through the binoculars.)*

MECKEL. Maybe is not good to keep strange, randomly appearing golem in house, you never know what golem he might –

*(**MECKEL** glances down at a toolbox.)*

MECKEL. Ey, is my toolbox!

HETCHMAN. See? Is good golem.

MECKEL. Didn't you tell me fucking Mendelssohn stole my toolbox?

(**HETCHMAN** *picks up a glass jar.*)

HETCHMAN. And look! Is past memory!

MECKEL. What?

HETCHMAN. Is past memory I thought I lost –

(**HETCHMAN** *puts his ear against the sealed jar. Out comes a memory: happy party music.*)

HETCHMAN. Is day I turn fifty-two.

MECKEL. Oh yeah, uh?

(**HETCHMAN** *puts the jar with a collection of other jars.*)

HETCHMAN. *(re: other jars)* Is time I win cool raffle.

Is time I make longest shit on toilet.

(**HETCHMAN** *opens the jar, waves it in front of* **MECKEL**)

MECKEL. Yep. I remember that.

(**HETCHMAN** *shows off the more recent memory jars.*)

HETCHMAN. Is time I win annual potato race.

Is time I am partially eaten underwater by small alligator.

Is time *you* get into unfortunate spat with my long-distance provider.

MECKEL. And golem: is finding my memories as well?!

HETCHMAN. Is probably just because you use my telephone on occasion.

MECKEL. Oh.

HETCHMAN. I go through them all later.

(**MECKEL** *scans the jars hurriedly for any* **MECKEL**-*colored jar.* **MECKEL** *picks up the small pink jar.*)

MECKEL. And what is this?

(**HETCHMAN** *grabs it from* **MECKEL**.)

HETCHMAN. Eh! Is nothing. Is time I – uh, vomit pink peppermint stick, is all. Is nothing.

(**HETCHMAN** *quickly hides the small pink jar.*)

HETCHMAN. So! Where you go now, uh?

MECKEL. *(re: flashlight)* Cemetery –

HETCHMAN. Oh yeah? You hear that, golem! We go to cemetery!

MECKEL. You are wanting to go out now?

HETCHMAN. *("yes!")* Is anniversary of dead people day!

(*The* **GOLEM** *comes out of the basement with its hat on.* **MECKEL** *is taken aback.*)

HETCHMAN. *(re: hat)* Is good look, uh? On big handsome over there!

(*The* **GOLEM** *blushes: "who, me?" The* **GOLEM** *exits.*)

HETCHMAN. Meckel?

MECKEL. Hm?

HETCHMAN. You okay?

MECKEL. Oh. Yeah. Am okay.

(**HETCHMAN** *and* **MECEKL** *exit.*)

VOICE. "Hetchman strolled to the cemetery with Meckel and this supposed stufffinder golem. It would be not until later that he would realize his mistake."

Scene

(Cemetery)

*(****HETCHMAN****, ****MECKEL****, and the ****GOLEM**** in lawn chairs, with the remains of lots of food. ****HETCHMAN****'s chair is well-equipped for a lawn chair, kind of like his living room chair. All are slightly drunk. ****HETCHMAN**** holds the flashlight. He is at the end of a familiar story.)*

MECKEL. Was not how it happen!

HETCHMAN. Oh really.

MECKEL. Was totally different!

HETCHMAN. Okay then, Mr. Big Hat:

You tell me

You tell me how it go.

MECKEL. Well, Hetchman he used to be a total big hat around town. Everyone they want to be like Hetchman.

HETCHMAN. Meckel was the nice one.

MECKEL. Hetchman was the hat one.

HETCHMAN. Is true!

MECKEL. Is how we got into all the parties.

'Cause you have party and you don't invite Hetchman?

Not having Hetchman would be like not inviting toilet to house.

Is just necessary!

'Cause Hetchman he don't like you? He don't make you hat?

You are fucked.

HETCHMAN. Nooo!

MECKEL. Yes!

HETCHMAN. Nooooooo!

MECKEL. Is true!

HETCHMAN. Okay, is true!

I don't like you – ?

Eh. You are small fucked.

MECKEL. All my life, I live in giant hat-shaped shadow of Hetchman.

HETCHMAN. *(modestly)* Eh.

MECKEL. But people today, they have no respect for the hat.

Now? Hetchman, he could be cat herder for all they care.

(HETCHMAN checks his watch, stretches.)

HETCHMAN. Boy, Doshka, she is taking long time to come down.

MECKEL. We give her a little longer.

HETCHMAN. *(to GOLEM)* His wife, Doshka she was so dumb!

MECKEL. *(shrugs)* She was spatially challenged.

HETCHMAN. But she was always a good wife, so easy.

MECKEL. Is sometimes easier to have occasionally dumb wife.

HETCHMAN. Doshka she never ask you for hat?

She never want to know what the hatmusic it sound like?

MECKEL. *(shrugs)* Doshka is Doshka.

Your wife, she is different.

(HETCHMAN checks his watch.)

HETCHMAN. Maybe Doshka don't want to say hi this year.

Our dead friends, they come out, say hi.

Even Schnell the gimpy baker dragged himself out here two hours ago.

MECKEL. Or maybe she is stuck in swamp.

She will come.

(A noise. MECKEL turns.)

MECKEL. Doshka?

Oh. Is just branch.

Is just shitting seagull on branch.

*(**MECKEL** tries to scare the shitting seagull away.)*

HETCHMAN. When she come, golem, I show you.

I show you how she is slightly stupid.

Golem. Golem?

*(The **GOLEM** is asleep. **HETCHMAN** chuckles, lowers the hat over the **GOLEM**'s eyes, and pats the **GOLEM** gently.)*

HETCHMAN. It is not so bad having small one, uh?

MECKEL. Is so and so.

HETCHMAN. But you and Doshka, you liked having small one, uh?

MECKEL. Is big mess, small one.

They sleep, they barf

They eat glue, they barf.

You have to clean sweater vest all day long!

You would not have liked it.

HETCHMAN. But you and Doshka, you have many small ones.

MECKEL. Is just not who you are, is all.

HETCHMAN. Whatchu mean by that?

MECKEL. You are not baby type, you know?

You are, uh, solitary man type. Like totem pole.

You do not have the love inside you.

Is okay!

Is not good, is not bad.

Is just who you are, is all.

HETCHMAN. You have always thought this?

MECKEL. *("yes")* Eh.

HETCHMAN. And my Whodoyoucallher, she think this, too?

MECKEL. Even Whodoyoucallher.

HETCHMAN. Oh.

MECKEL. Is just 'cause you never say how you love her, is all.

HETCHMAN. Whatchu mean by that?

I tell her I love her. I tell her –

(**HETCHMAN** *stops, tries to remember an instance.* **MECKEL** *falls asleep.*)

HETCHMAN. …long time ago.

(**HETCHMAN** *turns back to* **MECKEL**.)

HETCHMAN. Meckel? Meckel?

(**HETCHMAN** *sees that* **MECKEL** *is asleep, too.* **HETCHMAN** *takes out a paper and a pen. He begins to write.*)

WALL. HETCHMAN THINK FONDLY OF WIFE?

(**HETCHMAN** *sees the wall, nods.*)

HETCHMAN THINK FONDLY OF WIFE

Scene

(The train)

VOICE. "And that same night, hours later and still more towns over, Hetchman's Wife found herself once again on the train – "

(The hat sits on the train. **HETCHMAN'S WIFE** *returns to her seat on the train.)*

HETCHMAN'S WIFE. How you doing, hat?

You cold?

Is getting cold, uh?

Is good thing we are not still waiting outside fifth-best hatmaker's shop. Would be lousy thing to wait there, in the dark, dark cold.

(beat) The conductor, he tells me tomorrow, we will pass by the water.

What do you think it will look like, uh? The water.

They tell me it is blue.

Me? I am not so sure.

(beat) What does it sound like, the music?

(The hat says nothing.)

HETCHMAN'S WIFE. Is okay.

Is hard to say what you hold inside of you.

What it is I cannot hear.

Ey, hat.

Hat?

You asleep?

Okay, you sleep.

*(***HETCHMAN'S WIFE*** *sits and waits. She hears the rumbling noise in the distance. She listens to it, calm.)*

HETCHMAN'S WIFE. It will be soon.

(**HETCHMAN'S WIFE** *pats the sleeping hat, then realizes that there is an envelope next to/beneath it.*)

HETCHMAN'S WIFE. *(struck)* Mail.

Is for you?

(**HETCHMAN'S WIFE** *reads the label. Awestruck –)*

HETCHMAN'S WIFE. Is for me.

Scene

(Living room)

VOICE. "And after all the living returned from the cemetery, Meckel tiptoed into Hetchman's home."

(An empty living room. A click at the front door. **MECKEL** *enters. As quietly as possible, he examines the jars. He picks up one jar, quietly opens it. From inside the jar, he hears* **HETCHMAN.***)*

HETCHMAN'S VOICE. – Merry Hatmas to me –

– Merry Hatmas to me –

*(***MECKEL** *picks up another jar, opens –)*

HETCHMAN'S VOICE. Good Meckel

HETCHMAN'S WIFE'S VOICE. Kind MECKEL

HETCHMAN'S VOICE. Best-looking favorite Meckel!

*(***MECKEL** *keeps searching, finds a* **MECKEL***-colored jar.* **MECKEL** *knocks into the jars, making a loud noise. Before* **MECKEL** *can hide, the* **GOLEM** *bounds in, sees* **MECKEL***. The* **GOLEM** *tackles* **MECKEL***.)*

MECKEL. What the hat – !

(The lights turn on. **HETCHMAN** *enters from the bedroom.)*

HETCHMAN. Ey, is friend not food!

(The **GOLEM** *backs off from* **MECKEL***.)*

(Then **HETCHMAN** *sees the jar in* **MECKEL'***s hand.)*

HETCHMAN. What is that?

MECKEL. Oh, is jar, I don't know.

(The **GOLEM** *moans.)*

HETCHMAN. Golem say you are late night sneak.

You are late night sneak, Meckel?

MECKEL. What?! No.

You would take crap golem's side over me?

HETCHMAN. Just gimme the jar, Meckel.

MECKEL. But then you will open it.

HETCHMAN. And?

MECKEL. And you will see why I am shitty friend.

HETCHMAN. Then let us see why you are shitty friend.

(**HETCHMAN** *stares* **MECKEL** *down.* **MECKEL** *sadly hands the jar to* **HETCHMAN**, *who puts his ear against it: the memory of* **MECKEL***'s phone call with* **HETCHMAN'S WIFE.**)

MECKEL'S VOICE. You still have hat?

HETCHMAN'S WIFE'S VOICE. I still have hat.

MECKEL'S VOICE. He kind of deserve it, though. To not have hat.

WALL. HETCHMAN FORGIVE MECKEL?

HETCHMAN. You have known where hat is.

MECKEL. Eh.

HETCHMAN. And you think Hetchman he deserve to be without hat?

MECKEL. No! Is just then maybe you see.

You see what life is like without hat.

Then you see what a good wife she is, how she don't leave because she is so good.

HETCHMAN. She don't leave 'cause she's my wife!

She don't leave 'cause she's mine!

MECKEL. Or she don't leave 'cause she feel sorry for you!

She call me last week, she tell me I got to hug your smelly ass to the ground 'cause she know no one else will do it!

(**HETCHMAN** *knocks* **MECKEL***'s hat off.*)

HETCHMAN. Out.

MECKEL. Hetchman –

HETCHMAN. Out!

MECKEL. But wall say you –

HETCHMAN. Wall say I what?

(**HETCHMAN** *glances at the wall. The wall sadly says…*)

WALL. HETCHMAN FORGET MECKEL.

HETCHMAN. You hatfailure Meckel.

You no pension, never die never retire Meckel.

You early-dying wife chooser Meckel.

Now get out before I have golem eat your foot off.

(**MECKEL** *grabs his hat and scrambles to the door.*)

MECKEL. She only want a hat like yours.

A hat of her own.

HETCHMAN. She wear hat when I say she wear hat!

And I say she wear hat never!

(**MECKEL** *exits. The* **GOLEM** *moans sympathetically.*)

HETCHMAN. Whatchu looking at, crapface?

(**HETCHMAN** *spits at the* **GOLEM**, *who melts a little. Saddened, the* **GOLEM** *takes off its hat, scuttles away.* **HETCHMAN** *sits back down in his chair, sullen.*)

(*In another part of the stage, lights up on* **VOICE** *watching this scene.*)

WALL. BUT UNDERNEATH ANGER IS BIG SADNESS

HETCHMAN. Oh shut up, wall.

WALL. IS NOT YOU I AM TALKING TO YOU, HETCHMAN.

HETCHMAN. Then who? Fucking Mendelssohn?

WALL. IS NOT MENDELSSOHN

HETCHMAN. Then who?

VOICE. "Despite himself, Hetchman began to hear a faint yet familiar voice."

(**HETCHMAN** *hears her voice. Weird.*)

HETCHMAN. Wall?

VOICE. "Not the voice of wall, but of a young woman."

(**HETCHMAN** *sees* **VOICE** *for the first time.*)

HETCHMAN. Ohhhh.

VOICE. "And though he had last seen her a long time ago, he knew."

(**HETCHMAN** *finds the small pink jar.*)

VOICE. "Hetchman then took out a memory – "

(**HETCHMAN** *holds out the jar to* **VOICE**.)

VOICE. – and handed it to me.

WALL. YES

VOICE. Why?

WALL. SO THAT SMALL ONE KNOW WHAT HAPPEN TO HER LONG TIME AGO
SO SHE SEE WHAT SHE HAS ALWAYS BEEN WANTING TO KNOW
IS TRUE, UH?

(**VOICE** *stares at the jar.*)

VOICE. I can't.

WALL. BUT YOU WILL
IS GOOD THAT YOU WILL
TRUST ME

(**VOICE** *opens the jar. Flashback:* **HETCHMAN** *and his* **WIFE** *in their living room.* **HETCHMAN** *works on repairing a hat.*)

HETCHMAN'S WIFE. Ey, Hetchman! I am with child.

(**HETCHMAN** *stops. He must've heard wrong. Eh.*)

HETCHMAN. *(dismissive)* Oh, okay.

HETCHMAN'S WIFE. Ey, Hetchman! I am with baby.

(**HETCHMAN'S WIFE** *has a baby now.*)

HETCHMAN. Yeah, yeah.

HETCHMAN'S WIFE. Ey, Hetchman! We are with girl.

(**HETCHMAN'S WIFE** *now has a baby covered in a pink blanket.*)

HETCHMAN. You say something?

HETCHMAN'S WIFE. We are with girl.

HETCHMAN. We are almost senior citizen, we have baby now?

HETCHMAN'S WIFE. Yes. Golem of life, he has finally come to see us.

HETCHMAN. Just now?

HETCHMAN'S WIFE. Just now.

(**HETCHMAN'S WIFE** *places the baby in his arms.* **HETCHMAN** *is struck with wonder and fear. He has a moment with the baby, before the baby bursts into tears.*)

HETCHMAN. Okay!

(**HETCHMAN** *waits for his* **WIFE** *to take the baby. She does not.* **HETCHMAN** *holds the baby towards his* **WIFE***, the baby stops crying.* **HETCHMAN** *then brings the baby closer to him, the baby starts crying. Far and close, far and close. The baby does not seem to like being geographically close to* **HETCHMAN**.)

HETCHMAN. Baby, she does not like me.

HETCHMAN'S WIFE. What, you want I should get Meckel then?

HETCHMAN. What? No!

HETCHMAN'S WIFE. Maybe he show you how to love baby.

HETCHMAN. You want I should love baby? I love baby, is easy.

HETCHMAN'S WIFE. You sure?

HETCHMAN. Is easy!

HETCHMAN'S WIFE. Okay. I be in back doing shitwork. You call you need anything, okay?

HETCHMAN. Okay.

(**HETCHMAN'S WIFE** *sees* **HETCHMAN** *caring for the baby. For a moment, she is pleased.*)

HETCHMAN'S WIFE. Okay.

(**HETCHMAN'S WIFE** *exits.* **HETCHMAN** *places the baby within arm's reach. He pats the baby less…and less… and less, and turns his attentions back to the hat in need of repair.*)

(*Gradually, the baby floats up from the pink blanket and out of the living room. Fastforward in time.* **HETCHMAN'S WIFE** *enters.*)

HETCHMAN'S WIFE. Where is baby?

(**HETCHMAN** *looks around in the pink blanket. Hey! No baby.*)

HETCHMAN. Is, was right here.

HETCHMAN'S WIFE. HOW YOU LOSE BABY?!

How you –

How you –

HETCHMAN. I don't –

I don't know.

I'm sssor –

Sssor –

(**HETCHMAN** *leans forward, extending his arms, offering a hug? His* **WIFE** *does not move. He folds in his arms.*)

HETCHMAN. *(snaps)* I'm very tired, you know this!

I told you I am no good for baby.

I do not have the love inside of me.

Okay?

(**HETCHMAN'S WIFE** *looks at him. In a moment, all her possible options float before her eyes. She exhales.*)

HETCHMAN'S WIFE. Okay.

VOICE. "But in her heart, she knew – "

HETCHMAN'S WIFE. Was not okay.

Would never be okay.

VOICE. "And still, my mother stayed with him, despite the realization that – "

(**HETCHMAN'S WIFE** *is struck with a realization.*)

HETCHMAN'S WIFE. He will always love hat more than you.

VOICE. "That – "

HETCHMAN'S WIFE. You will stay with him because it is what you were meant to do.

VOICE. "And that – "

HETCHMAN'S WIFE. Your name will never be mama or grandma, but just... Hetchman's Wife.

(**HETCHMAN'S WIFE** *exits.*)

VOICE. "After drifting up and away from my parents' home, I float off until I am loved to the ground by strangers who take me in."

(**VOICE** *folds the piece of paper in half, puts it away, and narrates on her own. She stares* **HETCHMAN** *straight in the eye. He clutches the pink blanket.*)

VOICE. And years after he loses me, I look my father in the eye –

HETCHMAN. Yes?

(**VOICE** *waits*)

VOICE. – and feel nothing.

Because I am Hetchman's daughter.

And I do not have the love inside of me.

(**VOICE** *screws the pink jar shut. She disappears from his view.* **HETCHMAN** *still has the pink blanket in his hand.*)

Scene

(Living room)

WALL. IS NOT SO BAD TO BE FLOATED AWAY BABY

VOICE. From the moment I got here, you knew they were my parents.

WALL. ERROR OF OMISSION?

VOICE. So how did you do it? How did you get me to come back here?

WALL. IS NOT WALL.

VOICE. Oh really.

WALL. ALL THINGS THEY COME BACK TO WHERE THEY ARE FROM

VOICE. And what am I supposed to do with that? Now that I know?

WALL. OH SMALL ONE
IS NOT FOR WALL TO SAY

VOICE. Then who?

*(**GABE** enters from the bedroom.)*

GABE. So what do you want? To be left alone? Is that it?

VOICE. No.

GABE. Then why does it feel like ever since we've moved in here, I come into the room and it's like I don't even exist for you?

VOICE. Welcome to my world.

GABE. I make you feel like that?

VOICE. No –

GABE. *I* make you feel like you're nothing?

VOICE. I didn't say that. You're great! You're so great with me.

GABE. Then what is it? What do you want?

I thought I knew. I thought it was me and here and this.

But evidently that was wrong. So you need to tell me.

'Cause I can deal with your moods, I can deal with your insecurities, but I can't deal with not knowing. I just can't.

(beat)

VOICE. You love me, right?

GABE. Of course.

VOICE. And how do you know that?

GABE. Because I do. Because I always have.

VOICE. See, that. I've never felt that.

GABE. What do you mean?

VOICE. I am lucky. I am so lucky. But sometimes this doesn't feel like my life, sometimes it feels like I'm living this checklist.

GABE. Checklist?

VOICE. I get a job, I get a boyfriend, we move in together, I have what most people would kill to have. But I look at you and I don't know if I feel what I should. I don't know that I feel for you what you feel for me.

GABE. And what do I feel for you?

VOICE. Love.

GABE. *(question)* For me.

VOICE. For anyone!

GABE. So what: you don't like me? Is that it?

VOICE. What? No: I like you. I like you a lot.

GABE. But you don't love me.

VOICE. I'm not sure I would know what that even feels like. Or whether there's anything I can do about it.

GABE. And when were you going to tell me? When we got engaged? When we got married?

VOICE. You wanted to know. This is it. This is me.

See? Now you're mad.

GABE. I'm not mad. *(thinks)* No. Wait. I am mad.

I can be mad, right? 'Cause this is kind of shitty to tell someone this late in the game.

VOICE. I just didn't want to hurt your feelings…like I'm hurting them right now. I just wanted to give you what you needed.

GABE. I need to be with someone who loves me back. That's what I need. Which is actually pretty simple.

VOICE. No, it's not.

GABE. Okay.

(GABE *grabs his jacket.*)

GABE. You know what I'm going to do? I'm going to get in my car and I'm going to drive to my parents' house –

VOICE. And what?

GABE. I don't know. You don't know. And I don't either. And that seems kind of fair, doesn't it?

VOICE. Gabe.

GABE. And just remember: I don't need you to do anything for me. I want you, I like you, I usually love you, but I don't need you.

(GABE *exits.* VOICE *sits there for a moment. Then she rips up the papers in her hands.*)

WALL. EY!

EY NOW!

WHAT YOU DO THAT FOR, UH?

VOICE. This is my story. It's mine to do with as I want, right? You can send it down, but you can't force me to read it.

WALL. BUT IS STORY

IS STORY YOU HAVE ALWAYS WANTED TO KNOW

VOICE. And maybe that was a mistake. Because the only thing this has done is basically confirm what I've always known: that I'm just some loveless lonesome who'll feel this way for the rest of her life.

WALL. YOU THINK WALL MAKE BIG SHOW

JUST TO SAY YOU DO NOT HAVE THE LOVE INSIDE YOU?

YOU THINK THAT IS POINT OF STORY?

VOICE. Isn't it?

WALL. UNLESS YOU FINISH
HOW CAN YOU KNOW?

VOICE. I'm not sure it would make a difference.

WALL. IF YOU DO NOT WANT TO READ
OKAY
BUT NO ONE THEY BECOME BEST TYPE PERSON
UNLESS THEY KNOW ALL ABOUT WHAT IT IS
THEY COME FROM
AND YOU?
YOU ARE NO DIFFERENT

(The wall sends a page down. **VOICE** *accepts it.)*

Scene

(Living room)

(HETCHMAN *just as we left him, in his chair and clutching the pink blanket.)*

VOICE. "And just as Hetchman found himself the most alone he'd ever been, his wife returned."

(HETCHMAN'S WIFE *enters.)*

VOICE. "As simply and as quietly as she had left."

HETCHMAN'S WIFE. I get mail you send me.

(HETCHMAN'S WIFE *takes out the envelope.)*

HETCHMAN'S WIFE. You tell me to come back. So what is it you want me to come back for, uh?

(HETCHMAN *opens his mouth. No words come out at first.)*

VOICE. "Immediately, Hetchman's mind was flooded with a million things he might say to his wife."

HETCHMAN. His housecleaner

His shoegetter

VOICE. "Things like – "

HETCHMAN. No!

VOICE. "And – "

HETCHMAN. Clean!

VOICE. "And – "

HETCHMAN. Where you put my slipper?

VOICE. "But none of these seemed to express the bigness of his love, the utter – "

HETCHMAN. – hat shape of it! –

VOICE. "All he could come up with was – "

HETCHMAN. I…have run out of peanut?

HETCHMAN'S WIFE. I see.

(HETCHMAN'S WIFE *takes out the hat, hands it to* **HETCHMAN.** *)*

HETCHMAN'S WIFE. Here.

Is your hat.

I could not make same hat.

Happy?

(**HETCHMAN** *takes his hat and puts it on. His hatmusic plays: the most beautiful music in the world. It pours over* **HETCHMAN** *joyously.*)

VOICE. "Overjoyed by his hat's return, Hetchman failed to notice his wife's disappointment in their long-suffering, sad-thinking marriage."

(*Even in his rapture,* **HETCHMAN** *hears Voice's words. What did she just say?!*)

HETCHMAN. What? No.

Was not sad-thinking, was happy-thinking.

Was love.

HETCHMAN'S WIFE. Oh really?

HETCHMAN. (*remembers*) List! I make list!

All this time we have been married, I forget to say how I love you.

You must let me tell you list!

Okay?

HETCHMAN'S WIFE. Okay.

(**HETCHMAN** *reaches into his pocket, pulls out his messy, jumbled notes. He reads, flustered.*)

HETCHMAN. Uh, how I did not enter wife-beating contest, even when there was cool prize?

Is love!

HETCHMAN'S WIFE. Is laziness.

HETCHMAN. How you get out of car to check to see if I have space even though space it is six meters long?

Is love!

How I hold onto your purse when you are on toilet?

Is love!

How I tell you I have to fart when I have to fart?

Is love!

How I am okay with your face even now that you are big ugly?

HETCHMAN'S WIFE. When am I big ugly?!

HETCHMAN. Is recent development, is okay.

How you go to store and buy clothes for me? Final sale, no return?

Is love!

How long time ago, we go on honeymoon and we get sick of each other at exact same time?

HETCHMAN'S WIFE. Is love?

HETCHMAN. Is love of same amount!

Remember?

We sit in honeymoon suite and you say – !

(*Flashback to* **HETCHMAN** *and* **HETCHMAN'S WIFE**, *newly wed, holding each other's hands, very close together.*)

HETCHMAN'S WIFE. I am sick of you.

HETCHMAN. I am sick of you, too.

HETCHMAN'S WIFE. Just now?

HETCHMAN. Just now.

HETCHMAN'S WIFE. Me, too!

HETCHMAN. Same time!

HETCHMAN'S WIFE. You leave wet towel all over, is disgusting!

HETCHMAN. You grind your teeth at night, is so annoying!

HETCHMAN'S WIFE. Honeymoon, it will be over soon.

HETCHMAN. Yeah.

(*Ahhh. They move farther apart, but still hold hands.*)

HETCHMAN. How we go out and we wear same outfit without knowing?

(Flashback to **HETCHMAN** *and* **HETCHMAN'S WIFE** *in the male and female versions of the same outfit.)*

HETCHMAN'S WIFE. We are wearing same outfit.

HETCHMAN. Oh yeah.

You want I should change?

HETCHMAN'S WIFE. *("no")* Eh.

(back to the present)

HETCHMAN. How I lose things, how I lose your most important thing, and still, *still* you stay with me?

HETCHMAN'S WIFE. To stay is not to forgive.

And is love, but not love of same amount.

Can never be.

Goodbye, Hetchman.

HETCHMAN. Goodbye? But you have just come back.

HETCHMAN'S WIFE. Is time.

Golem it has come for me.

HETCHMAN. Golem? Is nothing!

Is just stufffinder golem, is all.

HETCHMAN'S WIFE. Is golem of death.

HETCHMAN. What?

VOICE. "And suddenly, Hetchman realized that his randomly appearing golem had not arrived for him but his wife. And not to serve him but to take her away."

(In another part of the stage, the **GOLEM** *waits. A rumbling.)*

HETCHMAN. No.

HETCHMAN'S WIFE. Hetchman: I am tired.

I have been tired for so long.

And now: I am ready.

You will be okay without me. I see you will be okay.

HETCHMAN. No!

(**HETCHMAN** *embraces his* **WIFE.**)

HETCHMAN'S WIFE. Let go, Hetchman.

Let go.

(**HETCHMAN** *lets go. He looks at her. This is the first time he sees how light and frail she has become. As if her body might disintegrate at any moment.*)

HETCHMAN. Wait.

Hat.

I make you hat.

I make you hat before you go.

HETCHMAN'S WIFE. You will make me hat?

HETCHMAN. Yes. So you stay, just a little bit longer?

HETCHMAN'S WIFE. I will stay. Just a little bit longer.

HETCHMAN. Okay.

HETCHMAN'S WIFE. Okay.

(**HETCHMAN** *takes off his hat, rolls up his sleeves, and hands his hat to his* **WIFE** *for safekeeping.*)

VOICE. "And with that, Hetchman went off to make a hat. Perhaps the most important hat of his career."

WALL. IS TOO SECRET TO SEE
SORRY

VOICE. "However, hours later, Hetchman reemerged with a hat. Not a man's hat, but a hat just right for a woman. For his wife."

(**HETCHMAN** *holds a hat. Not a man's hat, but a hat just right for his* **WIFE**. *It's like* **HETCHMAN**'s *hat in a weird way. She places it on her head.* **HETCHMAN** *watches his* **WIFE** *intently.*)

HETCHMAN. You hear anything?

VOICE. "As Hetchman waited for his wife to respond, a quiet kind of love washed over him. He remembered back to the first time he'd met the bright, beaming girl, the girl he once knew as – "

HETCHMAN. Hilde?

HETCHMAN'S WIFE. *(answering)* What?

HETCHMAN. Hilde. Is your name.

> *(**HETCHMAN'S WIFE** – now **HILDE** – realizes this is correct.)*

HILDE. Yes.

HETCHMAN. Has always been your name.

HILDE. It has.

HETCHMAN. Why did I not remember that sooner?

VOICE. "And then all at once, she felt it – "

WALL. THE MUSIC

> *(**HILDE** hears her hatmusic.)*

HILDE. Is this what it sound like?

HETCHMAN. What does it sound like?

HILDE. Beautiful.

HETCHMAN. Then yes.

> *(**HILDE** enjoys her hatmusic. **HETCHMAN** rolls down his sleeves, puts his hat back on. We hear **HETCHMAN**'s hatmusic again, but this time it's fuller, brighter. Their hatmusic combines to create one beautiful symphony. As they enjoy this –)*

HILDE. Ey, Hetchman.

> *(**HILDE** tips her hat at **HETCHMAN**.)*

HETCHMAN. Ey, Hilde.

> *(**HETCHMAN** tips his hat back. Eventually, they nestle together in **HETCHMAN**'s chair and listen to the music.)*

HILDE. What does it mean, the music?

HETCHMAN. It means we are happy.

HILDE. You are happy?

HETCHMAN. I am not happy but I am happy.

HILDE. Strange, uh?

> *(It grows darker. Whispers…)*

HETCHMAN. Hilde.

Hilde.

HILDE. What.

HETCHMAN. Nothing. I am just saying your name, is all.

Hilde.

My wife.

(**HETCHMAN** *falls asleep. The rumbling returns.* **HILDE** *gets out of the chair.*)

VOICE. "And late that night, my mother Hilde Hetchman was embraced by the earth.

Her life ended as it began:

With a hug."

(*The* **GOLEM** *embraces* **HILDE**. *She crumbles into the ground.*)

VOICE. "And even asleep, my father could feel his heart breaking."

(*Still asleep,* **HETCHMAN** *jerks up in his chair.*)

VOICE. "Because for him, there was no life after Hilde."

YES

(*The* **GOLEM** *sees* **HETCHMAN** *and takes him.* **HETCHMAN** *crumbles into the ground as well.*)

VOICE. "And suddenly all the love inside of my father, all the love that never surfaced during his life rose into the air with great force – "

(*the sound of something about to erupt*)

VOICE. " – until the very walls began to crack – "

WALL. UH HUH

VOICE. " – ripple – "

WALL. UH HUH

VOICE. " – and break."

WALL. BINGOOOOOO!

(The wall crumbles. No wall. **VOICE** *waits. A silence.* **VOICE** *sits down in the easy chair. She is completely alone. The feeling of this washes over her.)*

Epilogue

(Living room)

(Moments later, a knock at the door. **VOICE** *doesn't move, still in the chair.)*

(A man enters with a flashlight. It's **MECKEL***, even older than before.* **VOICE** *stares at him. He carries a package.)*

MECKEL. Good morning?

VOICE. Huh?

MECKEL. Is dark, but is morning. Me, I wake up so early now.

*(***VOICE** *stares at* **MECKEL***.* **MECKEL** *glances at the wall.)*

VOICE. Sorry. It just kind of happened.

MECKEL. Is okay. Wall like to make dramatic exit. But don't worry. Wall will always return.

VOICE. What are you doing here?

MECKEL. Oh! I am from next door. And I have package for you.

VOICE. For me?

MECKEL. Yes! Mail it has been waiting long time.

VOICE. I just moved in.

*(***MECKEL** *holds up the package.)*

MECKEL. Is your name?

VOICE. No, it's not.

MECKEL. You sure? I am thinking it is.

*(***VOICE** *looks at the package. "Miss Hetchman.")*

VOICE. Yes. That is my name.

MECKEL. Then is yours!

VOICE. But how did it – ?

MECKEL. Mail service is incredible thing!

Is super slow, but is always getting to the right person!

(**MECKEL** *hands* **VOICE** *something to open the box with.* **VOICE** *sifts through the package. She finds* **HETCHMAN**'s *hat and Hilde's hat, as well as the pink blanket. She dusts the hats off.*)

MECKEL. Oh wow. Is not every day you see hats like this. You wear it. It will look so good on you.

(**VOICE** *looks at* **HETCHMAN**'s *and Hilde's hats. Which one to put one? She chooses one to wear.*)

MECKEL. You wear one and you give other to boyfriend. Or maybe husband?

VOICE. I don't think he'd wear it.

MECKEL. No?

VOICE. I kind of fucked up.

MECKEL. Is okay. Marriage-related fuckup is most common fuckup of all. You will see.

VOICE. It's more complicated than that.

I'm not really sure whether we should even be together.

MECKEL. And this, it make you sad?

VOICE. *(thinks)* It does, but not like I thought it would. Isn't that strange?

MECKEL. Would you like to go for walk?

VOICE. I think I'm okay. Really.

MECKEL. Is anniversary of dead people today. Is lots of fun. Is time for all dead to say hi.

VOICE. *(struck)* Wait. That's today?

MECKEL. Oh yeah. My wife, Doshka, she is always super late, but every year, still I go. C'mon, maybe we see someone you know?

(**VOICE** *and the hats follow* **MECKEL** *out of the house and into the clear, warm morning. Dawn is breaking. The air is thick with presence of years gone by.*)

CPSIA information can be obtained
at www.ICGtesting.com
Printed in the USA
BVHW060526241221
624768BV00009B/675

9 780573 702846